S0-ACK-530

Alexander and the Wind-Up Mouse

All rights reserved. Published in the United States by Dragonfly Books, an imprint of Random House Children's Books,
a division of Random House, Inc., New York. Originally published in hardcover in the United States by Pantheon Books,
a division of Random House, Inc., New York, in 1969.

Dragonfly Books with the colophon is a registered trademark of Random House, Inc.

Visit us on the Web! www.randomhouse.com/kids

Educators and librarians, for a variety of teaching tools, visit us at www.randomhouse.com/teachers

The Library of Congress has cataloged the hardcover edition of this work as follows:

Lionni, Leo.
Alexander and the wind-up mouse / by Leo Lionni.
p. cm.
Summary: Alexander, the mouse, makes friends with Willy, a toy mouse, and wants to be just like him
until he discovers that Willy is to be thrown away.
ISBN 978-0-394-80914-4 (trade) — ISBN 978-0-394-90914-1 (lib. bdg.)
[1. Mice—Stories.]
I. Title.
76077423

ISBN 978-0-394-82911-1 (pbk.)

MANUFACTURED IN CHINA

48 47 46 45 44 43 42 41

Alexander and the Wind-Up Mouse

by Leo Lionni

Dragonfly Books New York

"Help! Help! A mouse!" There was a scream. Then a crash.
Cups, saucers, and spoons were flying in all directions.

Alexander ran for his hole as fast as his little legs would carry him.

All Alexander wanted was a few crumbs and yet every time they saw him they would scream for help or chase him with a broom.

One day, when there was no one in the house, Alexander heard a squeak in Annie's room. He sneaked in and what did he see? Another mouse.
But not an ordinary mouse like himself. Instead of legs it had two little wheels, and on its back there was a key.

"Who are you?" asked Alexander.

"I am Willy the wind-up mouse, Annie's favorite toy. They wind me
to make me run around in circles, they cuddle me, and at night I sleep
on a soft white pillow between the doll and a woolly teddy bear.
Everyone loves me."

"They don't care much for me," said Alexander sadly. But he was happy
to have found a friend. "Let's go to the kitchen and look for crumbs," he said.

"Oh, I can't," said Willy. "I can only move when they wind me.
But I don't mind. Everybody loves me."

Alexander, too, came to love Willy. He went to visit him whenever he could. He told him of his adventures with brooms, flying saucers, and mousetraps. Willy talked about the penguin, the woolly bear, and mostly about Annie. The two friends spent many happy hours together.

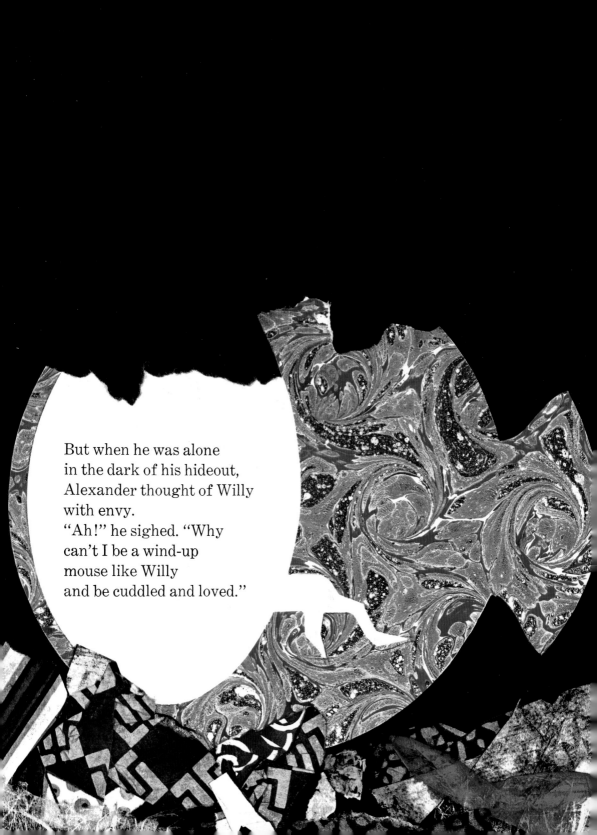

But when he was alone
in the dark of his hideout,
Alexander thought of Willy
with envy.
"Ah!" he sighed. "Why
can't I be a wind-up
mouse like Willy
and be cuddled and loved."

One day Willy told a strange story. "I've heard," he whispered mysteriously, "that in the garden, at the end of the pebblepath, close to the blackberry bush, there lives a magic lizard who can change one animal into another."

"Do you mean," said Alexander, "that he could change me into a wind-up mouse like you?"

That very afternoon Alexander went into the garden and ran to the end of the path. "Lizard, lizard," he whispered. And suddenly there stood before him, full of the colors of flowers and butterflies, a large lizard. "Is it true that you could change me into a wind-up mouse?" asked Alexander in a quivering voice.

"When the moon is round," said the lizard, "bring me a purple pebble."

For days and days Alexander searched the garden for
a purple pebble. In vain. He found yellow pebbles and
blue pebbles and green pebbles—but not one tiny
purple pebble.

At last, tired and hungry, he returned to the
house. In a corner of the pantry he saw a box full of
old toys, and there, between blocks and broken dolls,
was Willy. "What happened?" said Alexander, surprised.

Willy told him a sad story. It had been Annie's birthday.
There had been a party and everyone had brought a gift.
"The next day," Willy sighed, "many of the old toys were
dumped in this box. We will all be thrown away."

Alexander was almost in tears. "Poor,
poor Willy!" he thought. But then
suddenly something caught his eye.
Could it really be . . . ? Yes it was!
It was a little purple pebble.

All excited, he ran to the garden, the precious pebble tight in his arms. There was a full moon. Out of breath, Alexander stopped near the blackberry bush. "Lizard, lizard, in the bush," he called quickly. The leaves rustled and there stood the lizard. "The moon is round, the pebble found," said the lizard. "Who or what do you wish to be?"

"I want to be . . ." Alexander stopped. Then suddenly he said, "Lizard, lizard, could you change Willy into a mouse like me?" The lizard blinked. There was a blinding light. And then all was quiet. The purple pebble was gone.

Alexander ran back to the house as fast as he could.

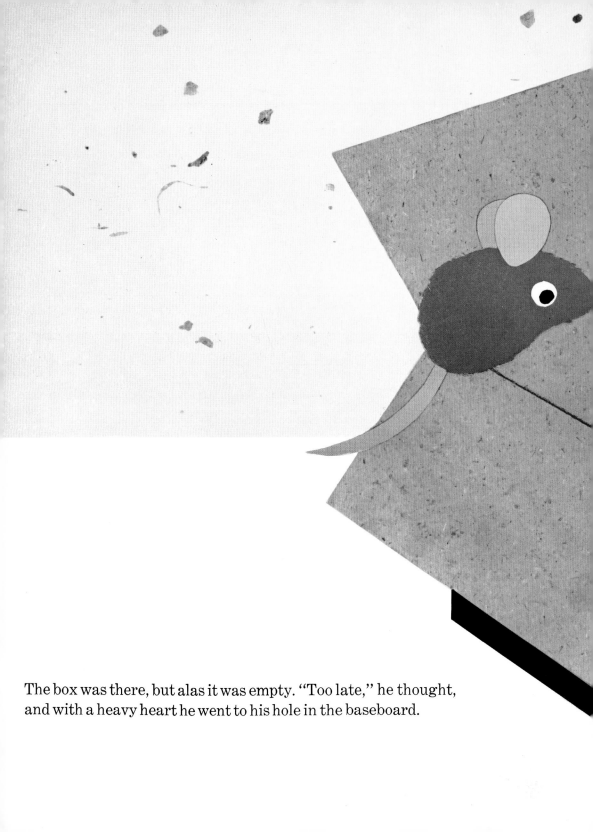

The box was there, but alas it was empty. "Too late," he thought, and with a heavy heart he went to his hole in the baseboard.

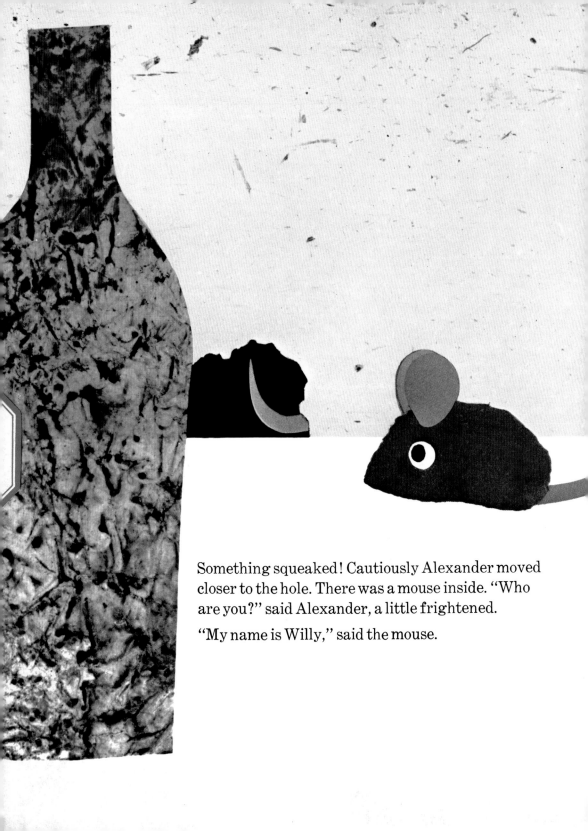

Something squeaked! Cautiously Alexander moved closer to the hole. There was a mouse inside. "Who are you?" said Alexander, a little frightened.

"My name is Willy," said the mouse.

"Willy!" cried Alexander. "The lizard . . . the lizard did it!"
He hugged Willy and then they ran to the garden path.
And there they danced until dawn.